I0760707

KRISTOPHER JEROME

THE GODS AND MEN CYCLE

WHITE WINGS FROM GREY ASH

A PRELUDE TO THE BROKEN PACT

White Wings from Grey Ash is a work of fiction. Names, characters, places, and incidents are the products of the author's imagination or are used fictitiously. Any resemblance to actual events, locales, or persons, living or dead, is entirely coincidental.

Cover art by Cristina Tanase.

Cover design by Miblart

Illustration by Patrick Buermeyer

Maps by Ralarismaps

eBook ISBN: 978-1-951138-08-0

Hardcover ISBN: 978-1-951138-09-7

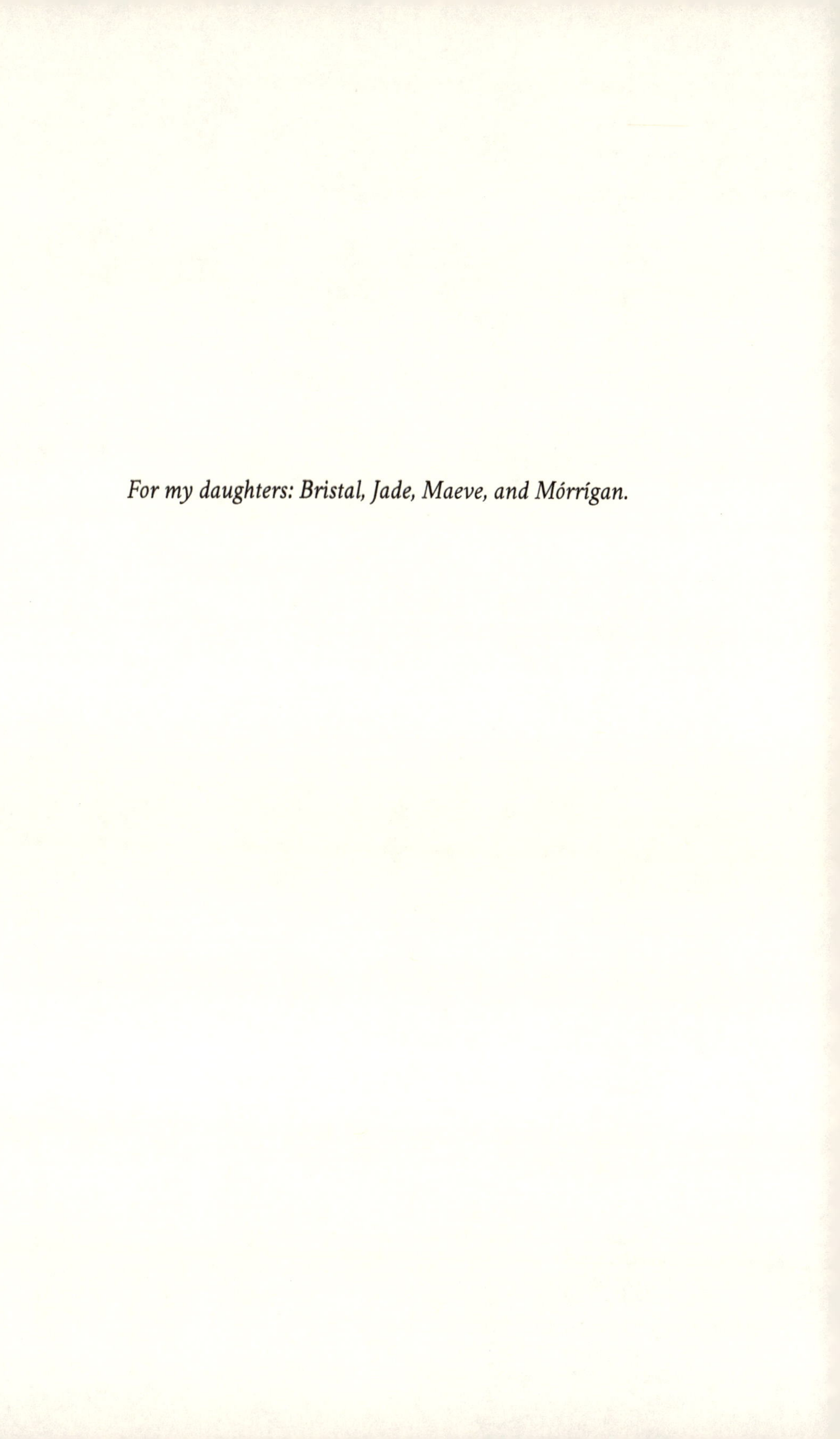

For my daughters: Bristal, Jade, Maeve, and Mórrígan.

ALSO FROM DARK TIDINGS PRESS

THE GODS AND MEN CYCLE

By Kristopher Jerome

The Broken Pact Trilogy:

- Wrath of the Fallen
- Cries of the Forsaken
- Tears of the Godless*

The Nightbreaker

White Wings from Grey Ash

Before the Breaking:*

- A Bandit's Balance
- A Voice from the Darkness
- In the Shadow of Light
- The Sons of Lighthammer
- The Bard's Demons
- Disciples of the First Cycle
- Ten of Seatown
- The Last Gift of Kane Darksend
- The Grey God's Edict
- The Blood-Soaked Sacrament*

*Forthcoming

Artorus
The Rim of Paradise
Lioss
The Grey Temple
Rinwaithe
Eligan
Dyeth
Seatown
Kliwen
Amel
Strega
Illux
The Great Chasm
Ostarth
Ryun
Firan
Marna
The Nameless Sea
The High God's Tears
Godsend

The Grey God's Shrine
Ayyslid
The High God's Throne
The Basin
Infernaak

WHITE WINGS FROM GREY ASH

PRELUDE

1034 AP

The ashes fell around her in clumps, drifting down from the grey above. They clashed with the snow, melting and mixing into a colorless paste that covered the ground of the plaza. Footprints and trails from the bodies drug along the ground crisscrossed this way and that, the vague remnants of the chaos that had broken out just moments ago.

Ren gripped the sword she carried tightly and exhaled. Everything was spiraling out of control. Even so, she would still do what needed to be done. She ran forward through the muck. Ahead, the door to the cathedral hung open, smoke billowing from within. She knew that the Seraph had been inside, planning the next stage of his conspiracy or praying for guidance. That meant that Arran was inside as well. The woman she had called sister.

She looked over her shoulder. The Demons were still attacking the barracks in force. Paladins and members of the City Watch weakly tried to rally a defense. The majority of their number were still hunting throughout the city, looking for *him*.

There is still time.

Ren passed through the smoke into the abattoir beyond.

1

1018 AP

Ren's parents had always done their best. They had never hit her that she could recall, nor did they raise their voices often, even when she deserved it. Yet they weren't always able to provide her with more than a single meal a day, and the winters were far too cold.

Life in the poorer districts of Illux hadn't been easy. Her mother was a washerwoman after an injury had removed her from a good career in the City Watch. Her father was a smith, though he seldom found enough work to keep his forge hot. It was for this reason that they had scraped together what little coin they could and moved out to Amel, a small village midway between Illux and Seatown to become farmers.

It had been nearly three years since that move, and still, they struggled to eat. Paladins protected the villages from direct raids by Demons and their Accursed minions, but bandits prowled the roads to the city, and often no Paladins were there to stop them. Few of the farmers that fed Illux were battle-hardened veterans. Ren's parents were better prepared than most, as each carried a sword at least. Ren had never seen either of them fight before, but she imagined that they were stronger than any bandit could hope to be. Even so, the danger often kept them from making this trip or earning money. They were forced to eat only what they could grow themselves, and during a harsh winter, that meant very little.

The wagon Ren sat in with the cabbages and beets bounced as it struck a hole in the worn road. Even as sure-footed as their donkey was, she doubted that she would be able to stay upright if they found a hole much bigger than the one they had just passed over. She was tall for her age, which meant that even sitting on the back of the cart, her long legs hung nearly to the ground. Absent-mindedly, she played with the fresh braids that her mother had woven into her black hair.

Ren's mother, Nirobe, walked on the left side of the donkey, her sword hanging loosely at her side. Nirobe had a limp from her time in the City Watch. The woman was stubborn though, so she chose to walk the entire distance to Illux rather than ride in the cart with her daughter. The guardwoman steadied herself with one hand on the donkey and the other gripping her polished mahogany walking stick. It had belonged to Ren's grandfather, a woodworker of some mild renown around Illux.

The staff was carved into the shape of each of the Seraphs. At night, after her mother would fall asleep, Ren would run her fingers over the smooth wood in the dark. She knew every face on the staff, and one day she hoped to learn the names of the figures her grandfather had carved.

Joran walked on the other side of the donkey, his fingers brushing that of his wife. He was an imposing man, at least a head taller than anyone else in their village—not counting the Paladins of course. Joran had a soft face though, for he never allowed a beard to grow. While Ren's mother had skin the color of almonds, Joran's was a shined ebony like her own.

As if he could tell that she was looking at him, the blacksmith turned and looked over his shoulder, casting a toothy grin at his daughter. She smiled back and then looked at the trail behind them.

I hope we get there soon. I want to see the city Paladins again.

The wilderness stretched on for miles, with no sign of human life other than the overgrown road that led back to Amel. Her father told her that it was safer to travel the road alone than with the larger shipments. Though there was strength in numbers, the bandits often knew when these larger groups were making the journey to Illux and planned accordingly. It was thought that each village had a least one or two spies for the larger bandit clans. Small wagons, taken by one or two families, would be more likely to go unnoticed he said. So far, he had been correct. They had yet to see anything dangerous during their trips between the two bastions of safety. Still, Ren's imagination played tricks on her, and she thought she could see armies of Demons and Accursed lurching out of each shadow.

Demon raids weren't common on this road—Amel was too close to Illux, at least when compared to other villages like Rinwaithe in the mountains or Marna to the south. Not since the Purge of Illux had Demons so openly stalked travelers of this road her mother had told her. Ren wasn't sure if that was true or not, for she knew that both of her parents would tell her small falsehoods to make sure that she wasn't afraid of the world. Like most parents that she had seen, they underestimated their daughter.

After several hours of traveling in silence, Ren's impatience got the best of her. She had been staring at her mother's walking stick again and figured that now was as good a time as any to ask questions about it.

"Mother," she said, "tell me about the faces on the walking staff. Which Seraph is which?"

Joran smiled. "Yes, my dear, give us a history lesson. It will make the time go by faster."

"Which face are you most interested in, sweet-thing?" Nirobe asked. "There are many Seraphs carved into the staff. Your grandfather spent years working on it—making sure that he captured the likeness of each one. He didn't know who would have need of such a beautiful walking stick until the day I was injured. On that very day, he had finished it, leaving one empty space of knotted wood beside Jerrok. The next Seraph can go there, if the walking stick outlives Jerrok, that is."

"I want to know about all of them!" Ren said excitedly.

"Why don't you start at the beginning, Nirobe?" Joran asked.

Her mother's face hardened somewhat.

"The history of the Seraphs is often dark, my child. They are great heroes, the very voice of the gods, yet they are human too—they fail in the same ways that we do. The first face, carved here," she pointed to a female face carved near the top of the staff, "is none other than Fiora Godschosen, the first of the reigning Seraphs."

"The reigning Seraphs?" Ren asked.

"Yes, love. Before the Pact, there were hundreds of Seraphs, all fighting to keep Illux safe from the Gods of Darkness. After the Pact, their number was reduced to one, who would rule Illux alone. Fiora was the first. She hunted down the Forsaken Ones and brought them to justice. She was noble and brave, and never ran from a battle."

"I knew that!"

"I'm sure you did. After Fiora was the Seraph Hector—"

"Wait, what happened to Fiora?" Ren asked, nearly leaning off the wagon.

"She was killed in a battle with the last of the Forsaken Ones, a rogue Seraph named Merek, who had once been the captain of Ash

Company during the Northern Campaign. He had been a great hero and friend to Fiora, and they died fighting over the sea. The Seraph sword Nightbreaker was lost, and not found again for quite some time," Nirobe continued. "As I was saying, after Fiora came Hector, who ruled Illux for a hundred peaceful years. By all accounts, he was a good man. The Fourth Spire was officially made the center of command for the Paladin Order under Hector. Then an army of Accursed and Demons laid siege to Illux and he was killed defending his people.

"A Paladin by the name of Millian was made the next Seraph during the siege. He fought back against the Demons and with the timely intervention of the Balance Monks, was able to save the city. During his reign, Illux tried to form an alliance with the Balance Monks, though it went against the edict of their Grey God. Finally, Millian was killed by a Demon raiding party when he was visiting the Grey Temple."

"The Seraphs die often, don't they?" Ren asked.

"Yes and no, dear," Joran said. "They have Divine Blood, so they do not age, and rarely take ill. But they can be killed, and the enemy eventually finds a way to do so."

"Always?"

"Always, child. Even Jerrok will die someday, though he will outlive all of us."

"I think that is enough for the moment," Nirobe said.

We didn't even cover half the faces!

"But mother—" Ren began.

"Shhh!" her father hushed.

Ren looked up and saw that there was a lone traveler coming down the road toward them. It looked like an older woman riding on a horse. Nirobe's hand tightened on Joran's. Her father set the palm of his free hand on the pommel of his sword. They didn't often meet travelers when they were bringing food to Illux. The sight of this woman seemed to put them all on edge.

As the woman got closer, she seemed to pay no heed to the small family traveling with their donkey and cart. Ren saw that while the woman's horse looked relatively clean and fresh, the old woman herself was dirty from head to toe. Her clothes were rotten, roughspun, and loose-fitting. When she was within earshot of them, the crone slowed her horse and pulled her shawl around her mouth—obstructing her face. Ren imagined that it was because she had rotten teeth that she didn't want them to see.

"Hello," she called, weakly.

"Hello," Joran said.

"Headed for Illux, eh?" the woman rasped.

"Aye," Nirobe said, gripping her staff.

"Talkative bunch you are. I expect such from stuck-up city dwellers in Illux, but not from farmers along the road. What are times coming to, eh?"

"My apologies," Joran said, relaxing and patting Nirobe on the hand. "We don't meet travelers often when we take this route. You can never be too careful. You just left the city, then? Was the rest of the road safe?"

"It was, it was," the crone chuckled. "I suppose you took me for a bandit or the like?"

"We might have," Nirobe said, still maintaining a chill in her voice. "Forgive me for asking, but what are you doing on the road alone?"

I wonder if she has seen a Seraph? She's old enough, maybe she saw the one before Jerrok!

Then Ren noticed something on the neck of the horse. At first, she thought it had been a small patch of mud, but she realized it looked almost like a red handprint.

"Who said that I was alone, my dear?"

The crone dropped her shawl, revealing that she wasn't a dirty old woman, but a dirty young one. Pulling two dirks free from her belt, she sprung from her saddle. The woman's boot slammed into the leg of Joran, sending him to the ground. She turned to face Nirobe, but Ren's mother was a moment faster. The ebony staff connected with the woman's face, sending a gout of blood and teeth flying. She stumbled backward, cursing.

"You fucking bitch!" she cried, covering her face. "Boys!"

Two large men on horses galloped from behind a copse of trees just off the side of the road. Nirobe tried to hold her staff out in front of her to menace them, but Ren could tell that without its support, her leg was failing. On the ground, Joran clutched at his leg, which was possibly broken. His eyes locked with Ren's. They seemed to be pleading with her: *run!*

Ren hunkered down in the wagon.

"Sweet-thing," her mother whispered. "You need to run. I will slow them down. All they want is our goods. They won't follow you. Run and don't look back."

Tears began to run down Ren's face. She couldn't leave them. Silently, she shook her head.

"Run!" Joran barked.

Her father tried to stand, but the wicked woman placed her foot squarely on his throat. She had removed her hand from her face by then, revealing a now crooked nose under all of the blood. When she next spoke, Ren could see that she was missing a few teeth from her upper jaw.

"Alright, you crippled bitch, I would have just taken what was in the cart and sent you running back to your village. Now, I'm gonna let these boys here rape you and your little whelp before I kill the three of you myself."

She spat a globule of blood onto Joran's face.

She was noble and brave, and never ran from a battle.

Ren watched in horror as her mother tried to swing her staff at one of the men. He grabbed the walking-stick-turned-weapon and yanked on the end of it. Her crippled leg finally gave and she lurched forward, falling into the mud beside her husband.

"Wait," the woman spat. "I want to have a got at her before you too have your fun. I know you won't mind."

She removed her foot from Joran's throat and kicked him in the face. He choked and wheezed loudly but didn't get up. The woman started for Nirobe, who was trying to stand.

She was noble and brave, and never ran from a battle.

Ren quietly slipped over the edge of the wagon and crawled to the side of her father while all of the bandits watched her mother struggle. His face was swollen and bloodied, but she knew he could see her.

"It's going to be okay, daddy," she whispered.

Tears formed in the corners of his eyes. He tried to push himself up but she held him down. With her free hand, she pulled his sword from its scabbard. It was a simple weapon, unadorned, but as sharp as any Paladin's blade. It was wickedly heavy for a girl of her size, but she didn't care. She had played with it before when her parents were both sleeping. This wasn't play, though. This was a battle, and she wasn't going to run.

Ren lifted the sword as high as she could and charged the woman. The bandit had just gotten to Nirobe and was bending down as she grabbed the woman by the hair. One of the men shouted something to alert their boss, but Ren couldn't hear anything but the blood pounding in her ears. The palms of her hands had gotten slick, so she tightened her grip. The sword was too heavy for her to swing, so she just pointed it up and pushed. The bandit woman spun around just in time for the blade to slide into her windpipe. She dropped her dirks and fell back into the mud, choking on her own blood.

The two men stood there in shock. Neither even thought to draw their weapons. Familiar hands pulled the sword from Ren's loose grip. She hardly noticed. All of her concentration was on the eyes of the dying woman. Those eyes were filled with hate, but soon that turned to fear as more blood seeped out of her neck. She tried to talk, but nothing escaped that gash in her throat. Ren finally looked up to see Nirobe standing again, sword in hand.

One of the bandits had already fallen, his body split at the shoulder. The other turned to get back onto his horse. Quicker than Ren thought she could move, her mother bent to the ground and grabbed one of the blades from the bandit woman and launched it through the air. The dirk took the last man right between the shoulders, knocking him from his horse. Ren had been so transfixed by the carnage that she hadn't noticed her father had drug himself to her side. She collapsed onto the ground into his arms, sobbing. She had killed a woman. She had saved her family, but she had killed a woman.

She was noble and brave, and never ran from a battle.

Nirobe wrapped her arms around them both, and the three of them cried. Later that day, when they began their journey again, all three of them were on horseback.

INTERLUDE

1034 AP

The smoke swirled around her face, clinging to her skin with heavy, warm fingers. The shouts from inside grew louder as she passed through the door. There were more people inside than she had been led to believe. It sounded like nearly a dozen warriors clashed in the central sanctuary.

The explosive power of the battle within reverberated throughout the entrance and beyond. The stones beneath her feet thrummed with expectant energy. Lightning crackled, fire roared, and above it all, people screamed.

Finally, she passed through the wall of smoke and ash, her dark skin glistening with sweat.

She was too late.

2

1030 AP

Ren didn't feel noble or brave. She felt like an idiot. Arran had bested her in combat again, as she seemed to nearly every time. The two fresh Paladins had been sparring in the training grounds just outside the Fourth Spire—the home of the Paladin leader in Illux: the Seraph Jerrok. The sparkling white stones of the five-spired Grand Cathedral loomed over them, covering the training grounds with its shadow.

Though they only used blunted practice blades, Ren was still sore from the beating that her companion had given her. Arran and Ren had been initiated together only a few months ago, though they had been close friends before that. After coming to Illux, Arran had become the sister Ren never had.

Ren had tried to enlist in the City Watch to make her mother proud, but she had changed her mind when she met Arran in a tavern one night. The other woman was loud and bawdy when she was drinking, but quiet and reserved when she was sober, or at least that was what she told the other patrons of the pub. Ren had encountered her somewhere in-between. After sharing a few drinks together, Arran told Ren that they would become Paladins together, much to Ren's confusion. The woman had sounded so confident that it was impossible to have doubted her. Right up until she vomited two days' worth of food onto the floor and got them both kicked out of the establishment. It wasn't until later that Ren learned that Arran had *the Gift.*

The Gift was a rare ability that allowed certain individuals to see glimpses of the future. Many claimed to have the Gift, but very few could actually prove it. Often, young soothsayers and old hags would claim the Gift and take travelers' money for fortune-tellings, laughing as soon as their unwitting victims were parted with coin. The High God only truly smiled on a chosen few, and Arran was one of those. She had seen that she and Ren would be initiated together, and, she claimed, she could see the outcome of every battle that she was to fight in. At least that is why she boasted that she could best Ren every time they fought.

Thank the gods mother didn't see that.

Arran reached down and offered a hand, pulling Ren to her feet. The other woman was petite for a Paladin; her bulk of muscles didn't look as inhuman as some of her brethren. She had a shock of bright red hair that she kept short but unkempt. Ren could never talk her into using a brush, even on initiation day.

"So, do you know exactly what moves I'm planning to use, or what?" Ren asked, exasperated.

"No, no," Arran laughed. "Nothing that specific. You know it doesn't work that way."

"It feels like it."

"I just get strong premonitions, feelings, for the most part. And usually, I feel like I'm going to win, so I take more risks. I figured you would have learned that by now."

Her chuckle turned into a belly laugh as she slapped Ren on the back.

"Sorry that you have to be on the receiving end all the time. I promise, one day you will—who am I kidding, I can't lie to you, sister. I love you too much for that. But I am sorry."

Ren smiled weakly, running her fingers back over the tight braids in her hair. She missed her parents. Both of them still lived in Amel, getting on in age as they were. Each walked with a limp now; each argued over whose was worse. They were proud of her, of what she was doing, but they would never live in Illux again. There were too many people here, and her parents disliked crowds. Perhaps, if she worked hard enough, she would get stationed at Amel. She doubted it, but one could hope. Until then, Arran was the only friend that she had. But that would be enough.

"Alright," Ren said, "did you see this coming?"

She twisted and tried to take a cheap shot with her practice sword, but Arran ducked away, still laughing.

"No, but you move so slow it didn't matter."

It was Ren who laughed next as she threw her practice blade onto the ground. She kept laughing, even as Arran stopped and weakly nodded behind her. Noticing that her friend's face went a shade paler, Ren spun around and saw a large group of Paladins making their way toward the pair. At their front was Castille, the highest-ranking and oldest Paladin in the order. Even with their prolonged lifespans, Castille was considered ancient. He looked old and weathered, though no less powerful than those around him.

"Are you recruits playing at being Paladins? Or are you Paladins that haven't learned decorum yet?" Castille asked.

Both women fell to one knee, bowing.

"Apologies, Commander," Ren said. "We were just practicing."

"The time for that is over," Castille said. "Come with me, you have been summoned to the Fourth Spire."

Both women stood.

"Not you," Castille said, pointing to Ren. "Just her." He jerked a thumb at Arran. "Jerrok wished to discuss her *gift.*"

He nearly spat that last word at them. It was no secret that the Paladin commander didn't believe in such nonsense. The only miracles he expected to see were those that came at the end of a sword. It was rumored that he would be the next in line to become Seraph if something were to happen to Jerrok. Woe to the people of Illux if that were to happen.

"With all due respect, Commander," Arran said, "I foresaw this meeting in my dreams last night. Ren was beside me when I spoke with the Seraph."

Castille clenched his fists and turned around, his retinue following him.

"Very well," he said. "Kane, pick some experienced warriors for the mission."

"Yes Castille," one of the other Paladins said.

His hair was dark and pulled back by a blue ribbon. The Paladin broke off from the others and headed for the barracks.

Ren shot a quizzical look at Arran. The other shrugged.

"Did you have a vision last night?" Ren whispered.

"I slept like a babe," Arran replied.

CASTILLE HAD LEFT his retinue in the small chapel at the base of the Fourth Spire, leading Ren and Arran up to the quarters of Jerrok alone. He didn't speak a word as they went up the winding spiral stairs to the Seraph's quarters above. Neither woman had been up here before. Most Paladins received their orders while they were practicing or staying in the barracks. Hardly any were called up to the Fourth Spire, the former temple to the Fallen One. How had word of Arran's gift made it to Jerrok's ear? What did he want from her?

She runs her mouth too much when she drinks.

Ren believed every word that Arran said about her visions and premonitions. She had never steered them wrong before. At least, not intentionally. They both agreed that the less other Paladins knew about her powers, the better. Neither of them needed the extra attention that would bring, and according to Arran, Ren had no choice but to be her friend through it all. Prior to finding Ren, Arran had been a drunkard who told everyone within earshot that she had the Gift. Now she was a drunkard who only told half the bar about it.

After an interminable amount of time circling up the steps to the spire above, they stopped at a landing with a giant oak door. The dark stain looked like the color of dried blood. Castille knocked on the heavy wood with a ponderous slowness. The thunderous sounds echoed up and down the stairwell.

"Enter," the deep voice of the Seraph said from within.

Ren's heart leapt into her throat. Just being around Jerrok excited her. She felt like the little girl who once obsessed over her mother's walking stick again.

Castille pushed open the doors and entered the cavernous room within. The large chamber was decorated with various sets of armor and tapestries showing Paladin and Seraph alike doing battle against the Forces of Darkness. One image, in particular, caught Ren's eye. Two Seraphs, a man and a woman, grappled over a body of water. It must have been when Fiora and Merek killed each other.

In the center of the room was a large table with a map of the Mortal Plane spread out across it. Jerrok leaned over the table, studying its surface.

The Seraph was an attractive man, dark of skin like Ren, with the white hair and beard that marked him as a bearer of Divine

Blood. His armor was freshly polished, so much so that even his wings reflected in the surface of his shoulder pauldrons.

"What is it?" he asked, never looking up from the map.

"My lord," Castille said, bowing slightly. "I have brought the Paladin that you requested. The one with *the Gift*."

The grizzled Paladin commander seemed like he was trying to keep the disdain from his voice, though he was failing miserably. Jerrok looked up then, his dark eyes passing over both women in turn. He stood up from the table and made his way around toward them. Ren felt herself quiver with each solemn step taken by the Seraph.

"Who is the other?"

"This is Ren," Castille said. "She—"

"I saw her in my dream, my lord," Arran said, cutting Castille off.

Ren could tell that it took every ounce of control that Castille had to not backhand her right there. Instead, he silently ground his teeth.

"This is what I brought you here to discuss," Jerrok said. "How fascinating that you dreamed of this meeting. I have heard tales of your gift. Did you know that one of the Champion Daniel's companions had this gift also? Springjack the Silent—a mute warrior who helped lead Daniel to greatness."

And to destruction.

Ren felt herself grow cold. Her mother's tales of the history of the Mortal Plane returned to her.

"I didn't realize," Arran said.

"Yes. Often do we sing of the greatest heroes, while forgetting those who helped them the most. Every child knows of Daniel, of Ash Company, or Arendt. But who mentions Springjack or Aryk? They are every bit as important to the continued existence of the Light as we know it. I called you here because I, too, strive for this same greatness. I wish to have the Light crush the Darkness beneath its heel like it once did, and I cannot have that without the aid of visions like yours.

"Tell me, what have you seen? I know that some doubt your gifts, but believe me, I do not."

Arran seemed to blush for a moment. She inhaled and then began, "Mostly they are feelings. Premonitions. But sometimes I do dream. Sometimes I do have the visions of which you speak. There is one that has consumed my nights since I was a child. I saw fire. Ashes fell from the sky like snow on a winter's day. They blanketed everything I could see. Then, a winged figure formed from the ashes rose up and led our people to a final salvation, free from the Darkness."

Ren looked at her friend with newfound awe. Arran shared most of her visions and premonitions, but she had never once mentioned anything this monumental. Was she telling the truth? Arran looked smaller all of a sudden, as if she was trying to hide within herself now that all of this had been brought out.

"Did you see who this figure was? Did you see their face?" Jerrok asked.

"I-I did not, my lord," Arran said, weakly.

"No matter. It must have been me. I knew that there would be something like this. Did I not tell you, Castille? Had they not already proclaimed this when I slew the Herald with the Lance of Retribution? I made the weapon mine, just like Nightbreaker!"

He was getting excited now, pacing back and forth around the table and map. Castille stood there silently, his face hardened like a statue.

"There have been setbacks recently. Seatown attacked again, this time by a Paladin no less, but we saw to that. This is exactly the sign that you and I have been waiting for."

Jerrok turned and walked back to the map. He motioned Arran over.

"Tell me, where will they strike next?"

"My lord, it doesn't work like—" Arran began.

Jerrok slammed his fist on the table. "We are going to make history. Use the gift you were given by the High God! He blessed you for a reason!"

Gods. What has she done?

Arran placed her hands on the map and closed her eyes. Suddenly, they snapped open.

"Amel."

No!

HER PARENTS HAD BEEN happy to see her, at first. And then she told them why she was there with a group of some twenty Paladins and a few dozen soldiers, too. No sooner had Arran had said the word "Amel" than Jerrok and Castille sent the two friends and a group of Paladins to the village under the command of a veteran named Kane.

Amel was nestled nearly halfway between Illux and Seatown, and as such, in many ways it served as a small travel hub between the two larger settlements. Word had been sent to Seatown to send any Paladins that they could spare, and to keep the rest on alert. Ren doubted any of the eastern Paladins would arrive, as they were still rebuilding from the attack at the hands of the rogue Paladin Cecilia, which had only been thwarted a few months back. She had led an army of bandits, razing one village to the ground before turning her sights to Seatown. The rumor was that Cecilia had been killed by her lover Broderick, who had vanished after slaying her. Ren hoped he would show up again. He had been one of the Paladins in charge of training her before her initiation, and he had taken Ren and Arran ranging a few times to hunt bandits. He was one of the best Paladins in the order, they said.

Kane and the majority of the Paladins had gathered in the Paladin retreat in the center of town. This building was meant to house the handful of holy warriors stationed here, not the multitude that Kane had brought. Still, it did have extra rooms for when Paladin ranging teams passed through town. The overflow was held in the inn next door, much to the chagrin of the owner, who wasn't to be compensated. The soldiers marched about the village streets on rotation, sleeping in homes that they commandeered when their watch was up. Everyone was asked to make sacrifices for the greater good. The village wasn't happy, but they were safe.

"How long do you plan to stay?" Nirobe asked.

"We, uh, don't know yet," Ren said, casting a glance at Arran, who merely shrugged.

"Why do they believe we are in any danger?" Joran asked. "After that rogue Paladin was dealt with, I didn't think there was much danger out here. Jerrok has kept the Demons and Accursed in check. The Herald hasn't been in ages. Why do we think anything would happen now? And here?"

"A hunch," Arran said, playfully.

You better be right.

Ren shot her an icy glance. Nirobe and Joran didn't seem to notice. Their conversation was cut short by a loud knock at the door. Ren jumped to her feet, starting to draw her sword. Joran annoyedly waved her back to her seat and went to the door, shaking his head. When he opened it, the large Paladin Kane stood there, outlined by moonlight.

"They have come," he said.

Ren and Arran nodded and moved toward the door. Ren tried to ignore the look of panic on her parents' faces. She hugged them before quickly following her commander out into the street. Once they were outside and making their way toward the central hub, Arran broke the silence.

"What happened?"

Kane stifled a chuckle. "I was prepared to think your gift a hoax. Castille would have been pleased with that turn of events, no doubt, though it would have disappointed Jerrok to be sure. But then, several of our scouts didn't come back. The first that did spoke of a dark tide washing over the hillside. It seems that they snuck through the Rim. Scores of them."

"Gods be good," Ren whispered.

"What is the plan, Commander?" Arran asked.

"We set in and hold them back. I will not meet them in the open field in the dark. Even if the moonlight holds, we would be outmatched. This is their time, not ours."

"I agree," Ren said. "But what of the villagers? We cannot let the enemy make it into their homes."

"Then fight like you have never fought in your life. Have either of you faced Demons or Accursed before?"

The women shook their heads.

"Prepare yourselves. The forces of the enemy are twisted and cruel. The very sight of them defeats the weak."

Kane Darksend was a man born of the inner city families. His lineage could be traced back to the time of Arendt at least, if not before. As such, he carried himself with a certain disdain for those of lesser families and origins, as did any who bore the names Darksend, Lighthammer, or Whitehorn. Even so, watching him bark out orders and send soldiers this way and that to prepare the streets of the village for a light siege was inspirational. Ren and Arran stood beside him, watching all of this unfold as if they were somehow now of a higher rank themselves. It was an odd feeling.

"Pretty nice, eh?" Arran leaned in and whispered. "Bet you

didn't expect to move up so quickly. Guess you should listen to me more."

"Your mouth is going to get us in trouble."

"You can thank me after we save your parents and your village."

Ren glowered at her friend, but remained silent. Kane had been ordered to keep both women close. It seemed that Jerrok had taken Arran seriously when she said that Ren was to be with her through all of this. How much of those details she had fabricated, Ren was unsure. Ren still felt uncomfortable about the ramifications of that exchange, even if it meant that it had—at least for the moment—made her parents and village safer. Castille was well known even among the recruits as being an ass, but seeing Jerrok behaving so erratically concerned her. Seraphs weren't as perfect as that little girl on the road assumed.

After all, didn't Arkos become a tyrant? Gods, I wonder what the Paladins under him saw leading up to that madness.

All of the villagers and livestock were brought into the central few blocks of the village, cramming themselves into homes and stables that were barricaded from the inside. Torches were set along every street around the outer rim of the village, illuminating any entry. The next set of streets was the opposite, plunged into pure darkness just beyond the farthest reaches of the faint light that bled from the torches. It was here that the soldiers lay in wait. Although Demons could see much better in the dark than a human could, they were relying on the light of the torches blinding them until it was too late.

It was a good plan, at least for the moment. But it left the villagers no way to retreat if it failed. Although they knew that the enemy was originally coming from the north, that didn't mean that was the only way that they would attempt to flood the village. The way that the scout had described the oncoming force as a dark tide did little to quell Ren's uneasiness. If there truly were that many

Demons and Accursed coming, they could easily surround Amel and overwhelm its defenders before they had a chance to rally together.

Kane had the three of them crouched on one of the main roads leading to the north. He reasoned that the enemy would still come this way; there was no way that they could know that the village was defended by more than the usual paltry bunch of Paladins, even if they found a few scouts in the fields.

The minutes they spent crouched in darkness passed slowly with little change. Ren could hear the heavy breathing of the soldiers ahead of her. If she could hear them, would the Demons—

"Move!" Arran shouted, tackling Ren to the ground.

Gouts of black and red flame lit up the darkened street. Men and women died in a conflagration. Those who weren't incinerated screamed and ran in circles as they tried to quench the fire on their bodies. The torches around the village flickered as a wave of bodies ran through the light. The rotten corpse-warriors known as Accursed limped into the village, swinging their sword arms with unfocused malice. Kane was up before Ren and Arran, yelling over the cacophony of fire and death,

"Form up!" He shouted. "Death is upon you! Face it with honor!"

He raised his sword and charged ahead, cutting into each enemy he came across while never slowing. To Ren, it was awe-inspiring. Then she was able to see what the Accursed looked like: their rotten, naked flesh, the blades cruelly grafted to their arms. Fear washed over her. Her mind jumped back to the sight of the bandit woman, choking on her own blood. Ren shook free from her thoughts and jumped to her feet, pulling Arran up after her.

"Don't even say it," Ren said.

Arran snickered and pulled her blades free. Ahead, some of the soldiers had already broken rank and were fleeing deeper into the village. The other Paladins tried to turn them around, but to no avail. The two women ran after their commander, screaming at the top of their lungs. Some of the retreating soldiers saw this and turned back to follow them.

Ren ducked under an errant swing from an Accursed and shattered its arm with the pommel of her sword. She followed that up with a kick that removed its head from its body. Beside her, Arran peppered the wall of bodies with blasts of blue light that incinerated everything they touched. All the while, Ren tried not to look at the beasts too closely. It seemed that for every Accursed they slew, dozens more poured through the ring of light into the village. Her stomach churned as she tried to forget that each of these creatures had been a human once, even if they had forsaken the Light.

It wasn't long before more soldiers and Paladins came to reinforce them, for it seemed that Kane had been correct and the Demons had not ordered their forces to circle the entire village. That could have been their downfall.

"Forward!" Kane called out, his dark hair snaking loose of his blue ribbon. "Don't let them push us back!"

Ren looked at Arran. Her companion nodded.

"Just like we practiced," Arran said.

Ren ran straight at her, jumping and placing her foot into her friend's cupped hands. Arran launched Ren over the top of Kane into the mass of Accursed beyond. Ren focused all of her magic into her fist, causing it to glow brighter than any of the torches. When she hit the ground, she punched straight down, releasing so much energy that the earth around her quaked violently. Dozens of the creatures lost footing and fell, where they were easily hacked to pieces by Arran and the other Paladins.

"Stop showing off!" Kane barked, though Ren thought she could see a smile hiding in the shadows of his face.

Ren laughed for a moment as she stood, thinking about what her parents would say if they had been out here to see this. Her laughter was cut short when she saw the flickering yellow of torchlight reflected on the shining black armor of a Demon. The first of the hulking brutes stepped into the ring of light with its fist raised and already glowing red. Ren had no time to panic. She threw up a protective barrier of magic just as the blast slammed into her, sending her flipping end over end and back out of the ring of light into the darkness. When she landed, the wind was knocked out of her, but she was otherwise unharmed. It felt like her use of magic had drained her more than the Demon's attack had.

That was foolish. I'm listening to Arran too much.

Ren shook the cobwebs from her head and stood back up, just as Kane got between her and the Demon to engage it directly. They each seemed to be an even match for the other, though the Demon was undoubtedly less tired than Kane. Ren noticed that the Paladin was carefully moving in a short circle, his back to the darkness outside the village, leaving him exposed. For the moment, nothing took advantage of this lapse in judgment, but that wouldn't last for long.

What in the High God's name is he doing?

Then she saw. Arran disengaged from the Accursed that she was fighting and sprang through the air, stabbing both of her swords into the neck of the Demon. Black ichor stained its red cloak as it shuddered and collapsed to the ground. Kane nodded quickly before spinning around. A shadow broke away from the darkness and knocked him out of view.

"No!" Ren shouted.

She ran forward, pushing by any soldiers or other Paladins that got in her way. If Kane fell, the others would surely falter as well. There was no one else who could keep the Paladins and soldiers together. If they broke, the home of her childhood would be razed to the ground. Her parents would die a horrific death. Ren would not allow that to happen. Not while she drew breath.

Ren swung wildly, cutting a swath through the shambling soldiers of the enemy. Now their grim visage no longer frightened her. After a few moments, she found Kan struggling under a Demon, his arm pinned by its sword. His offhand glowed with a white-hot light that burst out just as she arrived, slamming into the Demon with a supernatural force, temporarily blinding Ren. And yet, the Demon stood, unshaken. The Paladin must have been weaker than he thought. Kane cried out and prepared to attack again, just as the Demon raised its own hand to do the same. Without thinking, Ren tackled the beast, sending it sprawling from atop Kane into the dark beyond.

They spun, grappling with each other out past the wall of light. Where her sword went, Ren hadn't a clue. Instead, she used her fists to pummel the creature as hard as she could, hoping beyond hope that it would be enough. She was a little girl again, trying to save her parents from bandits on the road. She could feel the weight of dozens of Accursed moving close, pressing against her. From deep within its black shell, the Demon cackled.

Luna, Goddess of Light, protect me. Samson, God of Light, protect me.

Ren focused all of her strength into the magic that she called to her clenched fists, lighting the darkness with two points of blue fire. The energy raged through her like a river after an autumn rain, the strain of which was so great that she heard herself crying out in pain.

"Arra! Goddess of Light! Smite your enemies!"

With her right hand, Ren punched the Demon in the head, releasing all of the magic in that hand as she did so. The laughter stopped as its head was turned to ash. Without looking up, Ren lifted her left hand and released a torrent of blue flame in a circle around her, destroying all Accursed that were nearby. She nearly blacked out when a familiar hand caught her. Ren looked up to see the concerned face of Arran lit by the faint light of the torches.

"We must retreat," Ren heard her say. "Come, sister. Kane is pulling back."

The next few moments passed by in a blur. Arran led Ren back into the light and away from the fighting. A few of the Paladins and soldiers still tried to hold their ground, but it looked as if the Accursed were too many. Thankfully, Ren didn't see another Demon, though she wasn't sure if that was because there weren't any or because she was barely conscious.

"We each killed our first Demon. Isn't that great, sister?" Arran asked.

Ren couldn't form words, so she grunted. They passed into darkness again. The next thing she knew, they were in the center of the town, crouched inside one of the larger stables. Her parents were there, and so was Kane, though he seemed to be asleep.

"What shall we do?" A voice asked.

"They will be here soon. We must flee!" Cried another.

Ren shook her head and looked around the stable, the world coming back into focus. Her father was standing in the middle of the stable, arguing with another man. Her mother loomed over her, wiping her head with a damp cloth. Beside her, Kane was unconscious, with Arran touching him with faintly glowing hands. No doubt the other Paladin could fully heal his wounds, but she dared not waste the last of her strength in case they were attacked again.

"If we flee, we lose everything!" Ren's father shouted. "What of the others? What of the soldiers and Paladins who died to protect us, just now?"

The other man put his hand on the hatchet that hung at his belt. "What of them? Do you want to die here, Joran? You still have your wife and daughter, take that as a blessing and let us leave while we still have time!"

Ren had heard enough. She pushed herself upright, ignoring the protests of her mother and her own body. A rage boiled through her that she couldn't name the source of. She saw the faces of the men and women who had died out there. She remembered what it was like to work the fields that would soon be burning. She thought of herself as a little girl, dreaming of Seraphs and Paladins and playing in the very streets that now ran red with blood.

Ren shoved past her father and grabbed the other man by the throat, lifting him into the air. The other villagers in the stable gasped and then fell silent. Faintly, the sounds of clashing steel and the sounds of dying drifted in off the street.

"We will not be broken," Ren said through gritted teeth. "So long as the Paladins of Illux fight for you, you shall not break."

She squeezed his neck tighter, causing his face to turn from scarlet to purple.

"Do you understand me?"

The man nodded. Ren dropped him to the ground, where he writhed in the dirt, wheezing and sputtering for air. She ignored him and looked around the stable. Few were of fighting age. Most were too old or too young. All told, there were less than a dozen villagers there that she thought could even hold a blade properly.

It will have to be enough.

"Grab anything you can!" She shouted. "Be it an axe, a sword, or a scythe, put it in your hand. We will not cower here and wait for death, nor will we leave Amel to burn. Arm yourselves and follow me!"

She steadied herself for a moment, closing her eyes. She was still weak from expending all of that magic. Ren took a deep breath and looked at her parents. She saw both of them standing together, swords drawn. She couldn't tell which one of them looked prouder of her. Arran was standing by them as well, leaving Kane's fate to the High God. The other Paladin gave Ren a faint nod and drew her weapons. Ren turned and walked through the opening to the outside.

The night had quieted. The last of the Paladins and soldiers had either fallen or fled. It didn't matter. They would stand against this tide of Darkness just the same. The villagers filed out into the night behind her, some muttering, some crying, but all doing as she had commanded. Ren grabbed a young boy brandished a wood-cutting axe.

"I want you to go and grab everyone from the other buildings they are hiding in. Tell them what I said. The fate of Amel rests with us."

Ren took the axe from the boy to arm herself. He nodded and disappeared into the darkness. Ren and the others moved to the very middle of the village, forming a tight circle as they waited for whatever came from the night for them. Soon more villagers trickled in, some armed with real weapons, though most with simple tools. After a few minutes, the boy returned, and it seemed that most of the village was behind him.

Ren took a deep breath.

The Accursed ran at them from the shadows of the streets beyond, stumbling ahead as quickly as they were able. Still, there seemed to be no Demons urging them on. A fact that concerned Ren greatly. If all of the Demons had fallen, then what had overcome the other Paladins?

"Hold!" Ren shouted to her makeshift army. "Let them come to you!"

It didn't take long for the tide of Accursed to reach the villagers, swinging their sword-arms savagely. Ren and Arran easily cut them down as they came to them, but the untested villagers had a much harder time. For every Accursed that fell, one villager was also wounded or killed. They swarmed the people of Amel like locusts, but to their credit, the villagers did not break.

Though she tried not to, Ren couldn't help but look through the mass of fighters for any signs of her parents. She knew that whatever she saw was likely to unravel her. Though the light was poor, she thought that she saw a glimpse of her mother and father back-to-back, each making short work of any of the creatures that came near them. That is what she hoped she saw.

Suddenly, a cry rose up from the villagers. Not a cry of anguish, but one of victory. The waves of Accursed had slowed to a trickle, which was close to sputtering out. It seemed that they had possibly reached the end of the horde. It was in that short-lived moment of reprieve that the hairs on the back of Ren's neck stood on end. She looked to the sky and saw a winged silhouette hovering in front of the moon. Long robes hung suspended in the air, held aloft by leather wings that stretched out like a scar across the pale circle in the sky. Beside the thing, Aenna seemed to dim.

The Herald.

The villagers began to scream in fear. They had found what it was that had done in the other Paladins. With how much strength Arran and Ren had used up in the battles tonight, they would stand no chance against a bearer of Divine Blood such as this. Ren looked for her parents again, but didn't see them. The world wanted to fall out from under her, but she didn't let it. The Paladin closed her eyes for only a brief moment before launching a barrage of magic skyward. Gouts of blue flame arced toward the creature. It batted them away as if they were nothing.

Nearly as soon as her own attack had faded, another sprang up from beside her, where Arran stood. The other Paladin was barely holding herself upright, and yet she flung fire at the beast just the same as Ren had. Then came another attack from a street over, where some other Paladin still clung to life. Then another. The Herald batted each away in turn but did nothing else in response. Then Ren saw Kane beside her. His face was grim, but his eyes looked at her with approval. He launched his own assault on the winged monster. This time, when it was done defending itself from the weak magic of the Paladins, it flew out of sight.

Arran collapsed, with Kane catching her at the last moment. Ren soon followed, though her parents were both there to lay her down gently. The last thing she saw was their smiling faces.

"You did it," her mother said. "You saved us all."

INTERLUDE

1034 AP

Jerrok lay dead.

As did many others. The priests had been cut down, and the Paladins who had come to their Seraph's aid were barely holding their own. Demons were scattered about the floor in smoldering ruins.

Ren scanned the area, seeking out any other resistance, trying weakly to keep her eyes away from the body of the fallen Seraph, broken and twisted on the central dais of the chamber. He had been cut down while praying for guidance. Seeing him like this struck her with the magnitude of what she had been coming to do.

His eyes stared at her hauntingly.

Too late.

She wiped away her tears and went to work.

3

1034 AP

The enemy wasn't far away now. Jerrok himself was leading this force into the wilderness, where he anticipated meeting the Herald and the gathered Forces of Darkness. Ren knew that she would be tested in ways that she couldn't even imagine in the coming hours. Beside her, Arran rode on a pale horse, stroking the animal's mane to quiet it as the fear of bloodshed hung overhead. While normally confident and aloof, the red-headed Paladin was introspective today. She said that this skirmish would have monumental implications for the future of the Mortal Plane, yet she didn't know why. While it was probably just Arran's flair for the dramatic, this pronouncement filled Ren with a sense of foreboding that she couldn't shake.

It had been years since she and Arran had mustered the villagers of Amel to defend their homes from the impending destruction that the Herald was attempting to bring to them. The pair had been on many an adventure since then, but none held the importance of that night. Before then, Jerrok had only known her as the friend of Arran, the woman who they said had the Gift. But after Amel, with a recommendation from Kane for their valor, both Ren and Arran quickly rose through the ranks of the Paladin Order. They were given positions of leadership over recruits, they were sent on prime ranging missions into the Rim and elsewhere, and perhaps most importantly, they were privy to the council meetings of Jerrok.

This preference among her superiors is what allowed Ren and Arran to ride at the head of the column today, alongside Jerrok, Castille, and Kane. Over the last few years, Jerrok had brought the war directly to the Demons, fighting them on their own turf. He wished to make them answer for the attacks on Seatown and the lesser villages over the last decade. Every battle that Jerrok led was to make them pay for Amel. Some even went so far as to claim that the Light was close to defeating the Darkness once and for all. Some claimed that Jerrok was going to do what Arendt could not.

How quickly they forget what happened to him.

Behind them rode hundreds of Paladins and three times as many soldiers. Scouts had reported that the Herald was uniting a similarly-sized force in the wilderness near the foothills of the Rim. Seeing this as his greatest opportunity for glory yet, Jerrok had marshaled nearly every fighter in Illux and marched forth. They emptied out of the city and washed across the countryside with the winged-warrior in the lead. He even carried the Lance of Retribution on this day—the very weapon with which he had killed the previous Herald over one hundred years before.

Ahead of the army, the Rim of Paradise loomed in the distance, towering over the Mortals that sought to spill their blood at its feet. Ren figured these mountains were so awe-inspiring that humans would have worshipped them if the High God had not created the Gods of Light.

Many climatic battles had been fought here, and once the entire war between Illux and the Forces of Darkness took place within the confines of these snow-covered peaks. Now they sat unoccupied except for the Grey Temple of the Balance Monks on their eastern edge. Ren's eyes flitted in that direction, her thoughts turning to the agents of Ravim, and what they might be forced to do if Jerrok was *too* successful. She shuddered and tried to push the thoughts from her mind.

"We are close," Arran said, to no one in particular.

Castille snorted, but then coughed loudly in an attempt to cover his mistake. Jerrok turned and met him with a gaze that could have melted the front of his breastplate.

"Yes, of course. But what of the outcome of this battle? Are you still unable to divine that?" Jerrok asked.

"No, my lord," Arran answered. "But, one does not need the Gift to know that the High God smiles upon you. I do not see victory, but I don't need to."

Arran shot a wink at Ren. Kane rode up between them.

"We will win, as it was meant to be. These curs will break before our advance, and we will knock them back against the mountains," Kane said.

"Of course," Castille stammered out, his face flush.

"And you, Ren?" Jerrok asked, paying no heed to the embarrassment of his most seasoned commander.

"I pray for our victory," Ren said. "As I always do."

"Are you not certain of it?"

"I'm certain of nothing, my lord," Ren said, carefully. "Nothing but the High God's love and the bravery of our troops. That gives me strength enough."

The Seraph said nothing and turned his gaze back to the way ahead. Soon, Arran said. Soon they would meet the enemy, and then only the gods knew what would happen.

. . .

KANE'S HORN blast signaled to the troops behind them that they had found their quarry. Ahead of them, spread about the plains below the foothills of the Rim was the largest army of Demons and Accursed that Ren had yet seen. The scent of rotten flesh filled the air here. Even so, she took heart, for their army outmatched the enemy two-to-one. The majority of the Paladins were mounted on horseback, and at the sound of the horn, they formed a line alongside Jerrok and the others, preparing to charge headfirst into the enemy. The unmounted Paladins and the regular foot-soldiers gathered behind the line of horses, preparing to follow directly after the first charge. Jerrok pulled Nightbreaker from its scabbard on his saddle and raised it over his head.

"Do you want these beasts to raid our villages any longer?" He shouted.

"No!" Thundered the reply.

"Do you want these bastards to lay siege to the city of our forebears?"

"No!"

"Do you want to bring honor to yourselves in the eyes of our gods?"

"Yes!"

"Then ride with me!"

Jerrok sheathed Nightbreaker and raised the Lance of Retribution, spurring his horse onward into a gallop. The others quickly fell into line alongside him, their weapons raised with battlecries of their own. Ren found the words, "For Amel!" leave her lips with a fury that she rarely let loose. Beside her, Arran said nothing, but her eyes were hardened with hate.

In a matter of moments, the wall of armor and horseflesh met the barely prepared line of Demons and Accursed, shattering through them like they were water from the sea. Jerrok's lance broke the helm of a Demon, spilling blood and brain in every direction. Ren clipped an Accursed in the shoulder, splitting it to its navel. She cursed as she ripped her sword free, spraying her mount with black ichor. Beside her, Arran released a blast of magic that sent two of the rotten combatants flying through the air, now nothing more than smoking husks.

After the initial surge, the enemy seemed to collect themselves and push back, severing the legs of horses and pulling their riders to their doom. Jerrok spun his horse about and shouted for the others to follow. The mounted warriors disengaged where they could and rode around behind the wall of foot soldiers to regroup. Once there, those with wounded horses dismounted and prepared to enter the fray on foot with the others. The soldiers and Paladins rushed the oncoming Demons and Accursed, losing all semblance of order within moments.

Arran's horse collapsed once they were to safety, the poor beast heaving as white froth and blood formed at the corners of its mouth. The Paladin gave the animal just enough healing magic to mute its immediate suffering. Before Arran could head back into the fighting, Ren also dismounted, falling into step beside her.

"You aren't walking in there alone," she said. "I don't care if you know this isn't the day you die."

Arran smiled weakly and nodded. She opened her mouth to say something, but it was drowned out by the thunder of hooves as another charge of the cavalry began. Ren knew that this would likely be the last time before Jerrok and the other abandoned their horses as well. They would be no help once the Demons started using their fire to spook the beasts. As Ren followed Arran into the wall of rotten flesh, she scanned the skies for any sign of the Herald. Thankfully, the wings of the enemy did not block the sun yet.

Together, the two Paladins marched into the morass of surging bodies. Arran sprang ahead, attacking with each of her swords like she was in no danger. Ren tried not to roll her eyes. She had finally gotten used to Arran's confidence in the Gift, but in a battle like this? Was her future really that certain? Was anyone's? Just as the thoughts crossed her mind, a lumbering Demon jumped between the two women, grabbing Arran by the head like a doll. Ren's heart stopped. She thought, for a moment, that she could hear the sound of the other woman's skull crunching under the strain of the Demon's great fingers.

Ren leapt onto the Demon's back, swinging her sword down at its arm with all of her might. Blue flame engulfed her arms and sword as she did so, cutting through the Demon's armor. It stumbled back, a sound of shock escaping from inside its helm. The brute's grip loosened, releasing its prey. Arran spun then, laughing as she jammed both of her swords upward into the creature's chest. The tips of her swords sprouted just above Ren's legs. Swearing, Ren jumped down just as the Demon shuddered and collapsed.

"I hope that looked as magnificent as I thought—" Arran began.

"Enough!" Ren shouted over the din. "I'm not going to lose you to your own stupidity. Have you ever considered that you were wrong? Have you ever wondered if your visions weren't true?"

A blast of fire struck both women, sending them spiraling out of the thick of battle. Arran landed atop Ren in a smoldering heap. The wry smile on her face looked weaker than usual, but it still hung on.

"If you had shut up, I could have warned you," Arran said.

Ren ignored her and tried to see where the attack came from, but she couldn't sit upright. It felt like her leg might have broken.

Where is my damned sword?

Arran suddenly sprang to a crouch, standing over her fallen sister protectively. Her fingers curved into talons, and her hands started to glow a faint blue. Ren lifted her head to see two Demons and a band of Accursed converging on them. The look on Arran's face was one of fear, an emotion that Ren hadn't seen on her in years. Ren felt a sharp pain in her stomach. If Arran was afraid, there was something very wrong. The red-haired Paladin launched her magic at the Demons, who easily deflected the blue flames.

"No!" Arran shouted. "This is not the day!"

The monsters ignored her plea and advanced on the two women. Ren forced herself to sit up, probing her leg. It was twisted at an odd angle, but no bones had broken the skin. She tried to will her healing magic to life to mend what she could, but there was little effect. Still, the enemies came closer, even as Arran hammered at them again, with an even weaker burst of magic.

"Arra, Goddess of Light, protect us," Ren prayed.

Hooves began to thunder again, followed by the mournful blast of a horn. Ren turned and saw the answer to her prayer: Kane Darksend galloped toward them, a spear in his hand. He launched the weapon at the closest of the two Demons. It skewered the blood-red cape, pinning the creature to the ground. The Demon quickly tore itself free, but not before Kane was in the midst of the advancing group, hewing skulls with his sword. The Demon took a mighty blow to the neck, sending it to the ground. Kane flashed a quick look at Ren, his gore-covered face panic-stricken.

The Paladin jumped from his saddle, knocking the other Demon from its feet. He followed his assault with a barrage of flame in an arc that destroyed the Accursed in a cloud of ash. Without slowing, Kane pulled free his spear and jammed it straight down into the chest of the fallen Demon. Gripping the haft of the spear even tighter, he broke the weapon off at the chest and stabbed the creature again with the jagged edge.

Kane ran over to Arran, catching her just as she nearly collapsed. He knelt, lowering Arran to the ground beside Ren. His expression was almost caring. For a fleeting moment, Ren was reminded of her father.

"Look," he said, pointing at the sky. "Hope is not lost. Jerrok will make quick work of that beast."

Overhead, silhouetted by the sun and Aenna, two winged forms slammed against each other again and again. Suddenly, Ren felt weak. There was a sharp pain in her side that she hadn't noticed before. She looked down and noticed that she was stained with blood. Her sword was lodged in a gap in her armor.

There you are.

She never felt the bite of the ground as her head struck stone.

WHEN REN AWOKE, the bulk of the army had pushed ahead, forcing the Demons and Accursed into a full-blown retreat. The world was still spinning around her as she opened her eyes. Another Paladin was standing over her, healing magic seeping from his fingers.

Just ahead of where she was laying, Arran was standing beside Jerrok, with Kane once again atop his horse. Jerrok was handing Kane the Lance of Retribution. The dark-haired warrior nodded as he took the weapon from his Seraph.

"Use this to pierce the side of the enemy. Take the eyes from the Gods of Darkness, Kane. Bring me the head of the Herald, and we will cleanse the world of the stain of sin once and for all."

"Yes, my lord," Kane said.

As he turned his horse, his eyes met Ren's for a moment. She saw pride there. The Paladins nodded at each other before Kane made his way toward the hills in the distance. The last thing Ren saw of him was the blue ribbon that still held back his hair.

Seeing that she was awake, Arran left Jerrok and ran to Ren's side. Once she was there, Arran quickly pulled Ren to her feet, ignoring the protests of the Paladin who had been doing the healing. Ren's leg felt shaky, but she was able to manage.

"Okay, okay," Arran began. "I know I messed up. But really, you stabbed yourself. That's on you. Better weapon control, you know? What would your mother say?"

Ren's head was still swimming, so all she could manage was a weak laugh. Her side ached from the effort.

"While you were out, Jerrok nearly killed the Herald," Arran continued. "We routed the enemy, and Kane has been sent to finish that bastard off. Gods! This is an amazing day. Hopefully, you are ready to see Broderick again."

"What?" Ren managed to say.

Broderick was no longer a member of the Paladin Order. Some time ago he had joined the Balance Monks. What was Arran talking about? Before Arran could answer, Jerrok was walking up to them.

"Recovering?" he asked Ren.

"Yes, my lord," she said meekly.

"Good. I will have need of you both soon. We will regroup and follow the horde to the end of the Mortal Plane if need be. The Gods of Darkness have failed this day."

"Truly, you are Arendt reborn," Arran said.

Ren nearly recoiled at the name. What was Arran thinking? Even though Ren thought the words a mistake and the name an insult, Jerrok's smile grew larger. He drew forth Nightbreaker, looking over the blade as if he had never seen it before. The black metal sparkled in the sunlight like a shard of obsidian.

"I have always known that I was meant to finish what he started," the Seraph said. "And I will. With you by my side, I am unstoppable. The Mortal Plane will tremble before me. This blade will run red with the blood of our enemies."

What enemies do we have left?

"My lord!" A man shouted, riding up on a dirt-covered horse. "Our advance has been stopped! Balance Monks have blocked us from following the Demons any further."

"What in the High God's name are they doing here?" Jerrok snapped, all joy leaving his face. He pointed Nightbreaker at the women. "Did you foresee this?"

"No," Arran lied.

Broderick.

Almost as quickly as the thought of her former mentor flashed across her mind, Ren saw a large column of Balance Monks riding toward where they stood. Although he looked very different than she remembered him—his hair was now shaved off and his body was covered in swirling grey tattoos—Ren instantly recognized Broderick Breaksword at the front of the charge. The Balance Monks spurred their horses onward until they were surrounding the Seraph and his Paladins. A blatant lack of respect, Ren noted. Jerrok sheathed Nightbreaker.

Broderick jumped from his horse, landing softly in front of them. He wasn't as bulky as he had been as a Paladin, but even lean as he was, he still exuded raw strength. His cool eyes locked with Jerrok, and for a moment, neither spoke. Ren had heard that the last time either of them had seen one another it had been under much worse circumstances. The rumors had irked the Seraph, but they still passed the lips of Paladins deep in their drink.

"What is the meaning of this?" Jerrok asked, finally.

"You upset the Balance of the world, Seraph," Broderick said. "You know what you did. Was Arendt not a lesson to you?"

"Was that a threat?" Jerrok hissed, his hand tightening on Nightbreaker. "Do you come to purge us as your cult purged Illux all those years ago? Have you truly forgotten your oath to your gods?" Around them, the Balance Monks seemed poised to strike.

"I have sworn new oaths now, Jerrok. I stopped being a Paladin even before you sent your dogs after me. I stopped being a Paladin when I slew Cecilia by your orders. Now, I come to you at the behest of the Grey God, to ask you this one time, to stop. Return to your city. Don't make us repeat the past."

While he spoke, Broderick's eyes passed over Ren and Arran. Ren saw more than simple recognition flash behind those orbs.

"There! They have surrounded your Seraph!" A voice cried out.

Paladins and soldiers began to swarm the large gathering, weapons drawn. Castille shoved his way through the mounted warriors until he stood in the center with the others.

"Are you hurt, my lord?" he asked.

"No," Jerrok replied. "Broderick was just informing me of my momentary lapse in judgment. Supposedly, his god is offering us mercy if we turn back now."

Castille snorted. "He would have done better to send someone who wasn't a traitor. Shall I give the command, my lord? We can easily kill these curs."

Gods. Don't do this.

Ren groped for her sword, belatedly remembering that the last time she had seen it, it had been sticking out of her side. Her stomach churned as she realized that she wasn't sure which side she would fight for. She never would have considered for a moment that she would turn against the Light, but slaughtering these Balance Monks? Killing Broderick? It didn't seem right. Would that really serve the Light, or simply Jerrok's ego?

"That will not be necessary, Castille," Jerrok said, sheathing Nightbreaker. "We will return to Illux. Turn the troops around. Kane will find us."

The grizzled Paladin commander sneered at the Balance Monks as he shoved his way out of the circle of riders and back to the gathering of troops beyond. Ren felt all of the tension leave her body. She tried to get Arran's attention, but the other woman wouldn't look away from Broderick and Jerrok. The Balance Monk stood completely still, arms crossed. The Seraph still gripped the hilt of his word, though he left it in its scabbard.

"Well, Broderick?" Jerrok asked. "What says your god now? Will he let us return to Illux in peace?"

"Aye," Broderick said. "But I am to accompany you."

Ren swore that a lesser sword than Nightbreaker would have snapped under the strain of the Seraph's grip.

INTERLUDE

1034 AP

The first Demon noticed her. It cut down the Paladin it was battling and charged. Its black blade flashed, shattering the pew beside her in an explosion of wood shards.

Ren threw up a barrier of blue energy, shielding herself from the brunt of the flaming blast that followed. When it saw that its attack had done nothing, the Demon paused. She used the momentary hesitation of the creature to attack. Each strike of her sword against the creature's own rattled her body. But still, she pressed on.

"Ren!" A voice shouted.

She turned and looked over her shoulder at its source.

Arran was barely standing; her face was caked with blood and soot. Her green eyes flashed in a silent plea for help. Ren could tell that Arran was actually afraid. The Gift must have told her how this would end.

Ren flew through the air, blood filling the inside of her breastplate where a fresh dent had formed. The Demon was standing over her again, ready for another strike.

4

1034 AP

The long journey back to Illux had been the most uncomfortable of Ren's life. Jerrok and Castille had ridden completely in silence, leading the army alone with the two Paladin women and the Balance Monk following behind. While Broderick had tried to make conversation with his former pupils, fear of reprisal from the Seraph kept both of them from exchanging many words with the man. Occasionally, the steely glare of Castille fell upon them, while Jerrok purposely kept his eyes ahead at all times.

A light wind whipped through the grasslands here; an icy friend from the Rim. Winter was coming south from the white tips of the mountains. Ren figured that Illux had a few days at the most before snow would blanket the city. She could see the breaths of the horses thicken in the air. Thank the gods they turned back when they did. A campaign against the Demons in the snow would have cost more lives than any battle.

During the night, while the army made camp, guards were stationed around the Balance Monk to ensure that he remained "safe". After most of the others had turned in, Arran kicked Ren awake. As her eyes fluttered open, Ren saw her companion standing over her, already in her armor again. At first, she thought she must be dreaming—Arran never got up first.

"What—" Ren began.

"Just get dressed. If we are armed, the guards will let us through," Arran whispered.

"Guards?"

"Just get your ass up!"

Ren groggily complied, putting her armor on as quickly as she could with limited light. The two women quickly slipped out of their tent and made their way deeper into the camp. They snuck by the large pavilion belonging to Jerrok, avoiding the ever-suspicious eyes of the Paladins stationed outside. From there, they wound their way past burning fires and the occasional drunk. It didn't take long for Ren to realize what guards her friend had been talking about. The small area where Broderick was being kept was straight ahead, surrounded by four Paladins. As they approached, Arran stopped creeping and stood upright.

"Will you excuse us?" she asked the guards.

They shared furtive glances but didn't move.

"Did you mishear her?" Ren asked. "Arran, which one of these men did you see Castille executing for disobeying a direct order?"

Arran smiled and moved her index finger from Paladin to Paladin. Almost as quickly as the two women had arrived, the men stepped away to a safe distance without a single word.

Loyalty and fear go hand in hand under Jerrok.

"What are we doing here?" Ren finally asked as Arran kneeled beside Broderick.

"He isn't safe," she murmured.

"I know that," the monk said without opening his eyes.

Arran nearly jumped back. Broderick smiled and sat up,

crossing his legs. He still hadn't opened his eyes; a look of serenity played across his features. If he hadn't spoken or sat up, he would have looked like he was in the middle of a pleasant dream. Ren's eyes followed the swirling grey tattoos that crossed his body, creeping up his neckline to wrap around the back of his bald head. After a few moments of silence, his eyes snapped open.

"After all of the times we went ranging together, after all of the training I gave you, you two think I am so naive that I wouldn't know Jerrok and Castille would kill me if given the chance?" Broderick asked.

"Did we think that, *sister*?" Ren shot at Arran.

"No, of course not!" Arran blushed. "But I did see you...die."

"What?" Ren turned. "And you didn't say anything?"

The other woman put her hands up defensively. The moonlight softened the hard look on her face. Ren thought that she could see a sheen of sadness in her eyes. Broderick never moved, but his body did seem to become more rigid.

"Death is certain for all of us, even the Seraph. You both know my history. I made my peace with that long ago. Now that I serve the Grey God, death holds even less power over me." He looked up at Aenna longingly. "Besides, I know the fickle nature of the Gift. What you think you saw and what you actually saw are two different things."

"I know what I saw, Broderick!" Arran snapped. "It will be the weakness of Paladins that will be your undoing."

Ren suddenly grew uneasy. She looked around to see if any of the guards had moved back into earshot.

"The weakness of Paladins is the very reason I am who I am," Broderick said solemnly. "And yet, there is still a strength to your kind that I see hasn't completely fled the Order. I do not regret my time in service to the Light, any more than Ravim himself regrets his time as a God of Darkness. Your concern for my safety, even as

I come to you as an enemy, means that my training was not in vain."

"An enemy?" Ren asked. "You are not our enemy, Broderick. You're our friend!"

"I'm an enemy of Jerrok, and therefore of the Light. It wasn't that long ago that he tried to have me killed. I defeated many of my brothers and sisters to protect myself from the wrath of your Seraph. Jerrok is a threat to the Balance of the world. Yes, I am an enemy, though it is love that guides my hand, not hate."

"What are you saying?" Ren leaned in, her voice a hoarse whisper. "Is the Grey Temple planning another purge?"

"As of yet, no," he replied. "But do not forget that it was the friends of Arendt who slew him. The Balance must be maintained at all costs. This is the directive of not just Ravim, but the High God himself. I appreciate your concern for my safety, but it is unnecessary. Stand or fall, I do as the Grey God requires, nothing more. Now go, before the Seraph thinks you have betrayed him. Your death would not aid the Balance, but upset it."

He closed his eyes again but did not return to the ground. The chill of the air set in, and Ren felt herself shiver. Arran turned and stomped off, tears flowing down her face. Ren quickly followed after her. When they were halfway back to their tent, Ren finally grabbed her friend by the arm and made Arran face her.

"Why didn't you tell me that you saw this?" she spat under her breath.

"I-I didn't want to upset you," Arran's eyes fell. "I saw the night before the battle that Broderick would join us one day, and fall to the Paladins the next."

"What else did you see?" Ren gripped her shoulders harder. "What is Jerrok planning?"

"I don't know. I swear."

"What did you see?" Ren growled.

"It's my dream, Ren. It's happening. I saw fire. And death. I saw ashes falling onto the snow, and from them sprouted white wings."

THE REST of the journey was undertaken in relative silence. Arran tried to speak to Ren as if nothing was wrong, but Ren ignored her. She couldn't shake the feeling of impending doom from her mind. As such, she blocked her friend's playful banter with an icy wall of indifference. Ren was used to Arran knowing more than she was willing to share, a quirk of being burdened with the knowledge that the Gift gave her, but this? She had known of the possible ruination of the Paladin Order, and a second purging of Illux, and had said nothing. Ren had been right to distrust the aspirations of the Seraph, he was going to bring their world to the brink of destruction. Surely this went against the will of the Gods of Light.

Several days after the battle against the Herald and his forces, they returned to the golden gates of the city. Snow already blanketed the walls and fields for miles around. Kane had still not rejoined them, leading to even more uneasiness among those traveling at the head of the army. It seemed far more likely by the day that if he had been successful in his mission to kill the Herald, he had sustained a mortal wound doing so. Jerrok had asked the gods if they had seen his fate in the Basin of Aenna; as far as he was saying, they had not. Though Ren wasn't sure, for she now doubted every word that came out of the man's lips.

Once they were back inside the city, Broderick asked permission to pray to the High God in the Grand Cathedral. Jerrok had allowed it, but only with an accompaniment of Paladins. Castille, Ren, Arran, and the other ranking Paladins had been ordered to join the Seraph in the council room at the top of the Fourth Spire. These recent events needed an immediate, and *private,* discussion.

"How many Balance Monks reside in the Grey Temple?" the Seraph asked as soon as the door swung shut behind him.

"The most conservative estimates say that they don't currently number a thousand, my lord," Castille replied. "But we haven't been able to have an agent infiltrate their ranks in some time. It's possible they have more than that..."

No. This can't be happening.

"I don't want to hear what's possible!" Jerrok snapped, pounding the map upon his table. "I want to know what is *certain*! How many monks could we expect to fight if we laid siege to the temple? More than we have Paladins? Less?"

"Lay siege?" A woman called Krynn asked.

"How else would you expect us to handle the issue?" Jerrok asked. "They have sent a spy into our midst for one reason, and one reason only. They plan to stop our advance on the Forces of Darkness. They plan to repeat the Purge of Illux. You heard Arran, I am Arendt reborn, and these cowards plan the same response that they gave him."

"You are correct, of course," Castille said, his eyes falling to Ren and Arran. "Despite this, we cannot allow cowardice to take hold. We must act."

The Seraph turned his back to the table, lost in thought. Ren felt sweat begin to form on her brow. She had known that Arran was rarely wrong, but this time she had hoped. She looked to her friend's face, thinking she might see some salvation there. If Arran would share what she had seen, perhaps this course could be averted. They had to do something. Arran refused to meet her gaze. Ren would have to act alone.

"What do the gods say, my lord?" Ren asked, her voice cracking.

Castille looked as if he was ready to throttle her for breaking the silence. Jerrok didn't turn around.

"Samson and Luna are in agreement with my plan. If we want

to truly win this war, we need to remove the Balance Monks from blocking our path. Ravim will not violate his precious Pact to create more servants, so once we have slain the last member of the Grey Temple, nothing will be able to stop us from finishing the Darkness once and for all."

"Are you sure this is the right course of action?" Ren asked. She felt Arran squeeze her arm. She shook her off.

Jerrok turned and glared at her. "I am. Would you prefer that we continue to fight this war forever? Sending hundreds and thousands to their deaths because we lack the courage to act? Or would you rather hide here behind the walls while we wait for Broderick to bring his army into our city and slaughter our people? Make no mistake, even if we stopped attacking the enemy today, the die has been cast, the Balance Monks are preparing to bring us to our knees as they did five hundred years ago."

Ren swallowed hard. He sounded so sure of himself, he sounded so *right*. And yet, something inside her screamed that he was wrong. It was the duty of the Light to stand against the Darkness, but did they need to bring destruction to the world? Hadn't the High God himself created Ravim to prevent them from going down this path? Jerrok claimed that his plan would save thousands, but she had her doubts.

"Tell me, Arran," Jerrok began, "what have you seen?"

Arran paused, measuring her next words carefully. Ren knew her friend well enough that she was preparing herself to lie.

"I have seen the Grey Temple in ruins. Once their true enemy strikes at them, they will fall, and the war will once again begin in earnest."

"And what then?" Castille said, his usual disdain for the Gift missing from his voice.

"Then our people can finally be free…" her voice trailed off.

Why didn't you warn them? Why?

"What would you like us to do next, my lord?" Castille asked.

"Prepare the troops again. I don't care how tired they are, I want the army to begin marshaling, and quickly. We won't have much time to catch them unawares. Arrest Broderick, I will execute him this very day. He cannot be allowed to commune with his god and let him know what we are planning."

"No!" Ren heard herself shout. Arran grabbed her again, squeezing even tighter than she had before. Castille's jaw dropped. "You can't! This is a mistake, my lord. Broderick has done nothing wrong. It's not too late to turn from this course. We don't need more death, we don't have to—"

"Silence!" Jerrok shouted, his voice filling the room with a supernatural weight. Lightning began to crackle around his fingertips. "I will not allow any further insubordination. You are a fine warrior, Ren, but you are soft. Broderick dies today, as does anyone who stands against the word of the Light, *my* word. Now get out of my sight, you sit on this council no longer."

Ren turned and walked from the chamber to the stairwell beyond. She heard Arran try to follow.

"No," Jerrok commanded. "You are not to leave my side until this war is won."

As she continued to the steps, her mind raced. Surely, she had made the wrong choice. There was no way that this was what she was meant to do. The Gods of Light were for this plan, why wasn't she?

Two of the Gods of Light. Arra, it seems, thinks as I do. We are not butchers.

It was then that she knew what she must do. She looked outside at the white city below. Snow had begun to fall once more.

INTERLUDE

1034 AP

Ren rolled to the side, just as the big brute swung again, its sword crashing against the stone floor where she had been, sending a shower of sparks and stones into the air.

She sprang to her feet, slicing upward into the legs of the creature. Her sword glanced off the dark plate, but the force of her attack still unbalanced the Demon. It collapsed to its knees. Ren's next stroke hammered into the helm of the creature with a ferocity that shook her entire body. It crumpled and fell.

Ren turned and scanned the rest of the room. Arran was running and jumping from pew to pew as two Demons overturned them right behind her. Then she fell.

"Ren!" she cried again.

Ren sprang into the air, her arm already glowing bluish-white from the elbow down.

"Unhand her!" she yelled.

The Demons turned and hissed. Her magic blasted the first one back through the air. It landed against the far wall and slid down, a smoking ruin.

The second Demon rolled to the side, sending a lance of flame into one of the stained-glass windows above. The image of Arra floating over armies of Paladins shattered, the shards falling toward Arran.

She cried out one last time.

5

1034 AP

Ren stood at the far end of the courtyard. She had remained so still that the snow had begun to turn her black hair white. Opposite where she stood was the Grand Cathedral. Somewhere below the central spire, the Balance Monk Broderick was being detained. She knew that Jerrok would not profane such a sacred place by having him killed there. No, it was more likely that he would be taken to the walls of the city. Though perhaps they would hide him in the catacombs. A new chill wracked her body, and not from the cool of the air. If that was the case, she would very possibly miss them altogether…

Her fears were for naught. Within moments she saw the monk walk down the steps of the cathedral, surrounded by Paladins. Jerrok was not yet with them, which meant that she still had time to act. There was still the possibility that Arran's vision could be averted. She tried not to retch.

There was no turning back from this moment. She risked losing her place by the High God's side if she did this. She remembered herself as a little girl, killing that woman who would have murdered her parents. She remembered the fear she had felt. And she remembered what her mother had told her of Fiora, first of the ruling Seraphs.

She was noble and brave, and never ran from a battle.

Ren waited until they were halfway across the courtyard when she broke into a sprint and charged. In her hand was a practice blade; her real sword would stay in its scabbard. She was doing this to prevent killing, not to be a killer. Not today. The other Paladins didn't notice her as quickly as Broderick did. When their eyes met, the Balance Monk nodded. He slipped the bonds that tied his hands as if they had been nothing. Lightning fast, Broderick punched the nearest of his captors in the small of the back so hard that their armor dented. The Paladin cried out and fell, just as the others drew blades.

Ren jumped then, her fury escaping her lips as a battlecry. The practice blade came down into the shoulder of the Paladin woman before her, teetering the woman off balance. Broderick swept the woman's legs out from under her, sending her to the ground beside the other fallen warrior. Ren twisted to the side, hammering one of the Paladins with a burst of blue flame. The man flew backward into a snowdrift, his smoking armor melting his surroundings into slush.

The two final guards sprang for Broderick at the same time, ignoring Ren for the moment. The grey monk ducked under one blade, twisting the weapon free of the man's grip. The sword fell into the snow with a muffled crunch. Then came the snapping sound as the man's arm was broken at the elbow. Ren winced and tried to ignore the crimson that began to stain the ground. The wound had been non-lethal, at least.

Her blunted weapon met the sword of the final guard in the air, just before it would have cut Broderick across the back. The force of the Paladin's attack snapped the practice sword in two. Ren felt her resolve failing as she looked at the man's face. It was twisted into a hateful snarl.

"Traitor!" he hissed.

The word cut Ren deeper than his weapon would have. She paused long enough to get struck backward by a burst of magic. She tumbled end over end, collapsing facedown in red snow beside the most grievously injured of the Paladin guards. Ren tried to stand but slipped on the slick slush beneath her. Broderick was there suddenly, lifting her to her feet. Together, they began running across the plaza. The man who had called her a traitor was facedown in another pool of red snow.

Ren's stomach churned even worse. What had she done?

Behind them, a horn blasted. More Paladins were running from the cathedral and the barracks across the plaza to see what the commotion had been. Thankfully, the fugitives reached the streets to the inner city and were able to disappear into the crowd coming and going from the early-morning religious services. When Ren looked over her shoulder, she saw a winged shape leaving the upper reaches of the Fourth Spire.

AN HOUR LATER, they crouched in an alley near the border of the slums, catching their breath. Neither had spoken since the battle. Ren wasn't even sure if she would ever be able to speak again. She was no longer sure that she was doing the right thing. What did she think would happen? Was she still a foolish little girl who thought that she could save her friend without anyone getting hurt? Her mind kept wandering back to the pools of red that stained the snow at the base of the Grand Cathedral.

"They live," Broderick said, as if reading her thoughts. "Killing them would have done nothing but enflame Jerrok more. I take it that you are privy to his plan? Was I to be executed?"

Ren nodded.

"So Arran was right, at least for the moment. Was this simply the grudge that he still holds, or something more sinister?"

Her tongue stuck to the roof of her mouth. She inhaled deeply before speaking. "He plans to move against the Grey Temple. Jerrok was going to kill you before you could warn Ravim. He wants to march on the Balance Monks today. I spoke out, and he kicked me off his council. And Arran..."

"And you threw everything away to save me?" Broderick asked, a smile crossing his face. "Or perhaps you serve the Balance more than you thought? I told you that I wasn't afraid of death, Ren. The only reason I fought them was to ensure that you weren't captured as well."

Ren broke down and began to cry. Broderick reached over to comfort her, but she shook him off.

"I'm sorry, Ren," Broderick said, softly. "I told you I was an enemy. I'm glad that you saved me, but I never wanted you to put yourself in danger like that. You and Arran both seek to influence the course of history, just as Jerrok does. Make no mistake, what the Seraph does will upset the Balance of the world. He risks the High God's wrath."

"No," Ren said. Her tears had stopped. "You aren't my enemy, Broderick. Jerrok is."

Ren stood, brushing a fine layer of snow off of her armor. She gritted her teeth as a group of Paladins ran down the street. The way they were moving made it seem likely that they were looking for her and Broderick. Once they passed, she leaned out of the alley to make sure that no other Paladins were near.

"Come with me, Ren," Broderick said. "We can journey to the Grey Temple; you can join us. Jerrok must be stopped, and as a—"

"You are right," Ren said. "Jerrok must be stopped. Can you make it out of the city on your own?"

Broderick nodded.

"I will look for you by the High God's side," Ren said. "Remember the people, Broderick. You fought for them once. They don't deserve the fate that your god would visit upon them. Hopefully, no more of them will die to feed Jerrok's desire for conquest."

Without waiting for another word from him, she ducked into the street and started running back toward the center of the city.

REN HAD to hide from Paladins on the lookout for her another three times before she returned to the plaza. It seemed that every Paladin in the city had been sent on the hunt. That meant that none of them would be between her and the Seraph.

No one but Arran.

Was this the dream that her friend had seen? Perhaps it wasn't Jerrok that was going to bring chaos to his people. What if it was her? She was about to engage in the ultimate act of heresy. She was going to try to kill her Seraph, and most likely die in the attempt. She swallowed hard. It didn't matter. She was on this path now. Arendt had done the same—led a rebellion to overthrow a corrupt Seraph. Ren nearly laughed. Arendt wasn't someone she wanted to compare herself to. No matter how this ended, she would be killed for treason. Perhaps she should have joined the Broderick and gone to the Balance Monks?

No. I fight for the Light. Even now. If Jerrok is dead, maybe this madness with the Balance Monks can be stopped.

Ahead of her, standing on the steps of the Fourth Spire was a lone Paladin. Before she even knew who it was, Ren drew her sword. She held no practice blade this time. She only wanted one death today, but her heart told her there would be several. How quickly she changed from trying to prevent any killing earlier.

Then she saw who it was that stood before her, and her heart caught in her throat. It was Castille.

"Well?" He asked. "What is it? Have you found your *friend*?"

"My friend?" she questioned, confused.

"Are you truly as thick as you appear?" Castille asked as he walked down the steps. "Or have you not heard? The Balance Monk escaped captivity. Five Paladins were seriously injured. The Seraph has ordered every Paladin in the city to be on the lookout for him."

"I-I had not heard," Ren stammered, sheathing her weapon. Castille eyed her suspiciously. "Was he alone?"

"Yes? Who else would have helped him?"

Ren lifted both of her hands and hammered him with a blast of energy as white as the snow that blanketed the plaza. The Paladin commander slammed into the doors behind him, and was knocked unconscious. Ren stepped over him, rolling his body down the steps with a firm shove. She opened the doors to the spire and ran inside, making her way toward the steps as quickly as she could. For the next few moments, at least, she had the element of surprise on her side.

She ran through the chapel that had once worshipped the fallen god Lio, where her initiation had taken place. The sounds of her footfalls seemed to mock her as they bounced back off the stone walls.

The Fourth Spire was eerily silent, save for her. Taking the steps two at a time, Ren sprinted up and up to her ultimate fate. She hoped that the Seraph would have cooled to her by now, allowing her to more easily take him unawares. With any luck, Arran would stay out of it altogether. Otherwise…

When she finally reached the heavy door to the council chamber, she paused one final time. If she turned back now, she could leave the city and catch up to Broderick, keeping some semblance of her honor. She would be able to see her parents again.

I can't.

The lives of those in Illux were still in danger of being ended by the Grey God's command, or Jerrok would march upon the Balance Monks and thousands would still die. There was no choice.

She was noble and brave, and never ran from a battle.

With a heavy heart, Ren knocked on the oak door.

"Enter," a deep voice called.

Ren pushed the door open and entered the room. Arran stood in the corner, looking as if she was trying to hide in the shadows behind the imposing Seraph. Jerrok loomed over the map of the Mortal Plane, troop markers pushed against the Grey Temple and Seatown.

Is he planning to attack Seatown after the Grey Temple? Why would he move his army over there as well?

The Seraph didn't look up.

"You still haven't seen any visions pertaining to Kane?" he asked distantly.

"No, my lord," Arran said, her eyes pleading with Ren.

"Pity," he said, looking up. "Why have you returned, Ren? I should have you jailed for even supporting that craven. Broderick nearly killed his guards and is on the run throughout Illux."

"I heard. Castille told me on my way up."

"You didn't answer my question."

"I came to protect the people of Illux from the slaughter."

Jerrok's confusion played across his face for just a moment before it was knocked away by rage. Ren sprang onto the table, slamming a blast of flame into the Seraph with one hand while swinging her sword down with the other. Jerrok didn't have time to draw Nightbreaker, so he reflexively blocked her assault with his forearm. The steel bit into his armor, drawing silver-red blood that dripped onto the map of the Mortal Plane. His magic flared to life, blocking the majority of her flames. The resulting conflagration caught the map beneath Ren's feet on fire.

The Seraph roared at the sight of his own blood. Ren pulled free her sword and swung again, this time catching him in the wing. Jerrok stumbled back, still barely mounting a real defense. She had caught him so off guard that he didn't know what to do. Nightbreaker finally made its way out of its scabbard, lightning arcing down its edge. Behind her, Ren heard the door fly open.

She ignored it and jumped.

Arran struck her from the side, tackling her to the ground. The two Paladins rolled across the floor to the feet of Castille and two other Paladins. Ren tried to stand, but a heavy boot crushed her arm. Arran wrestled Ren's sword from her, tossing it aside. Ren's stomach sank. She had missed her chance, and now she would die. Worst of all, her friend had betrayed her.

The Paladins accompanying Castille lifted her to her knees. The Paladin commander motioned, and Ren's captor on her right struck her across the face. He punched her again and again until she could barely hold her head up. Ren wasn't sure if the whimpering she could distantly hear was from her or Arran.

"Stop," Jerrok commanded. He walked forward and lifted Ren's face with the tip of Nightbreaker. "I want the city to see her death. Find me Broderick, so that they can die together. Arran, follow me to the central chapel. I want the pray to the High God." Then he leaned in close so that only Ren could hear him. "You are weak. The Light cannot bear your weakness. After we purge the Grey Temple, I will purge the Light of weakness such as yours."

Jerrok nodded, and the two Paladins drug Ren down the stairs. She didn't cry as she was taken away, but she did pray.

. . .

OUTSIDE, the snow was still falling. The cold felt harsh against her bruised face. Ren still wasn't allowed to walk, though she did feel some of her strength returning. At first, she had accepted defeat and prayed to the High God for forgiveness. Then, halfway down the spiral stairs, her resolve returned. Death was not her only option. At some point, she would be presented with an opening to escape, and she would take it.

I won't bow to your injustice.

A scream interrupted her thoughts. Ren turned toward the sound. A man was running from a building on the edge of the plaza. Behind him, orange light emanated from within the windows, dancing along the white canvas of the ground. Then a flame burst out to greet the cold winter air. The Paladins dragging Ren stopped to evaluate the situation. Suddenly, the man running from the burning building was incinerated by a burst of red energy. A dark shape jumped from a nearby rooftop and landed where the man had been standing. Another followed, and another.

Ren's heart sank. Somehow, Demons had made it into the capital unmolested, and all of the Paladins were searching for Broderick. She felt her Paladin guards release her as they drew their swords. Ren stumbled into the snow, falling like a child's discarded doll, left behind during a bandit raid. The cold bit her face. More shouts greeted her ears.

The imprisoned Paladin sat up, her captors barely taking note. Several members of the City Watch rushed into the plaza, weapons drawn. The band of Demons charged forward, sending blasts of magic flying into stray people and buildings alike. More fires broke out around them. The two Paladin guards sprinted to meet their new enemies head-on. Suddenly, the Demons split up. Half ran toward the Grand Cathedral, blasting out stained-glass windows with fiery bursts. The other half engaged the two Paladins, who found themselves quickly overwhelmed.

Ren ducked back down into the snow, praying that they would ignore her. Members of the City Watch ran by, screaming as they fled from the chaos. They were not prepared for Demons within the walls.

A few more moments passed in unsettling silence. Ren sat up again, looking around. The snow was crimson in several places, and a black plume filled the sky from the Grand Cathedral of all places. Flames sprang out from the upper floors, and ash fell from above. On the far end of the square, the other half of the Demon band was attacking the Paladin barracks, drawing away attention from the Grand Cathedral.

Ren gritted her teeth and searched for a weapon. She found a sword lying on the ground near where the charred remains of her captors lay. She said a prayer to Arra as she picked up the blood-slicked blade. Turning, she stared at the Grand Cathedral, the immensity of what she must do weighing on her again.

There is still time to do what needs to be done.

She could not allow the Demons to defile this holy place any longer, nor could she leave Arran alone in there. But she also couldn't forget the evil that Jerrok himself was about to engage in. One way or another, the Seraph would die today.

INTERLUDE

1034 AP

Arran twitched again, the blood draining from her body faster than Ren thought was possible. She smiled weakly up at Ren, but the light was quickly leaving her eyes.

"Don't," she whispered, sensing Ren's intent to heal her. "You need to heal yourself. Catch that Demon. It was the one that killed Jerrok."

"I can't let you die," Ren said.

"You must," Arran said. "Today is the day. I'm sorry, Ren. I never doubted your motives. What you tried to do was just, but I couldn't let you stain your honor. I've known all along. The vision I told you about. It was you. You are our salvation. You will rise from these ashes and lead our people into a new age of peace. You and him."

Tears began streaming down Ren's face.

"Who?" She asked.

"The boy," Arran said.

Then she was gone.

Ren let her friend slump back to the floor, her hair soaking up the blood that pooled beneath her. Ren closed her eyes and focused the healing magic toward the wound on her side. After a few moments, she felt the skin stitch itself back together, though her body felt weaker from the exertion.

The Paladin stood and sheathed her sword. The Demon had fled the Grand Cathedral after the death of Arran. No doubt, its companions that were providing the distraction by attacking the barracks were dead or gone. The assassin would be trying to flee the city by now.

I can't let it escape. It will kill others.

Just then, the room filled with Paladins and members of the City Watch. A bloodied Castille stood at their head.

"What in the High God's name happened here?" he shouted.

Then his eyes fell on the mangled body of Jerrok. Castille screamed. He ran to the side of his Seraph and fell to his knees, openly weeping.

"How could this have happened?" He asked through sobs. "Where were his guards? Where were the rest of you?"

"Nearly everyone was hunting for the Balance Monk, my lord," a man replied. "We were defending the barracks and the other structures around the area as you commanded. The inner city families were in—"

"You failed him!" Castille shouted, slapping the man with a gauntleted hand. Then he saw Ren for the first time. "You. Chain her! Chain the traitor!"

Ren allowed them to bind her, but she locked eyes with the man who would likely be the next Seraph. He broke his gaze from hers and exited into the roiling smoke.

6

1034 AP

Her cell was cold. That was what she hated the most. They were keeping her imprisoned beneath the barracks until the ceremony to make Castille the next Seraph was over. Then, imbued with silver blood, the new Seraph would publicly behead her and continue with the plan of his predecessor to attack the Balance Monks.

Ren's betrayal had been for nothing. She had thrown her life away for absolutely nothing. It hadn't even been her who had slain the would-be tyrant. The Demons had seen to that. No, Ren had simply stood against her leader and destroyed her honor. Now she would pay the price.

I should have killed Castille when I had the chance. That would have made a difference.

From the chatter outside her cell, she knew that Broderick had not been found. The search for the Balance Monk had been interrupted as soon as the smoke in the plaza had been seen. It also sounded as if the Demon who had killed Jerrok and Arran had escaped as well—after leaving a trail of bodies in its wake. Though she didn't truly regret turning against Jerrok, nor did she regret saving Broderick, each death caused by that Demon weighed on her. If she had simply gone along with the Seraph's plan, possibly each of the fallen would have survived, for the Paladins would have been able to muster a more coherent defense.

I deserve to die for that.

The only thing that brought her any semblance of hope was the thought that her parting words to Broderick might have in some way saved the people of Illux from another purge. Even with Castille marching on the Grey Temple, perhaps the monks would show mercy after beating back their attackers. One thing was certain now: with Broderick warning them of the impending attack, there was no way that the Light would overcome the children of Ravim.

Ren stood and started pacing around the room, trying desperately to regain some warmth. They had stripped her of her armor before throwing her in here, leaving her in only her underclothes. She eyed the reinforced door for a fleeting moment. If she really wanted to, she might have been able to blast it open. Little good that would do. The guards would have made short work of her after that. Her life, like the plaza above, was in ashes now.

You will rise from these ashes and lead our people into a new age of peace.

Arran's words came back to her again. The last vision that her friend had spoken of had supposedly centered around Ren. She didn't see how that could have possibly been true. Not now. Perhaps this boy Arran had mentioned would be the real savior. Arran could have been wrong. Perhaps it was all meaningless. If Arran had been right, surely things would be different.

"You don't give yourself enough credit," a voice said.

Ren was so startled that she nearly fell over as she spun around. There was no one in the room with her.

Oh gods, I'm losing my mind.

"No, you are not," the voice said.

"Where are you?" Ren shouted.

"I cannot go to where you are physically, not yet. It is forbidden."

"I don't understand."

Ren's eyes flitted around the room, but she saw no one. The guards outside hadn't seemed to notice the presence of the second voice. Even though it tried to reassure her, she still thought that she was losing her mind. The voice sounded like it was in the room with her, but it *felt* like it was coming from inside her.

"You know me, Ren. I am the goddess Arra, to whom you have prayed since you were a little girl," the voice said.

Ren nearly collapsed. The weight of those words came crashing down on her, along with the realization that they were true.

"But why? How? The gods cannot interact with any save the Seraph...So why me?"

"Haven't you realized yet, Ren?" Arra asked, her voice echoing like distant thunder. "You have been chosen. The three of us have taken turns choosing who is to become the next Seraph since Samson first chose Hector to rule after the death of Fiora. With the passing of Jerrok, the choice is mine. And I have chosen you."

Ren fell to her knees.

"The Pact forbids us from coming to the Mortal Plane, except in this one circumstance. When we are to give our blood to our next champion. If you accept, you will become the voice of the gods. You will lead the people of Illux until your death, may it never come."

"But why me? Castille—" Ren began.

"Castille," Arra interrupted, "is a loyal warrior, and a fine commander, but he is weak, Ren. Ambition has crippled that man beyond repair. He would rule like Jerrok. Worse than Jerrok. He would give the families of the inner city power over all in Illux. While Samson and Luna favor him for his predilections toward conquest like Jerrok, I do not. I see the desire of those men as a stain on the Light. Once we tried to crush the Darkness, cut it out root and stem, and that very penchant for destruction, that *blood-lust*, is what caused Lio to fall.

"Remember, the Pact was not created because of the actions of the Darkness, but of the Light. And though I do not agree with all of his pronouncements, Ravim does carry out the will of the High God. The Light should be caring, the Light should inspire hope, and provide protection from the Darkness, not the subjugation of the entire Mortal Plane."

Ren was shaking now. She was finding it hard to process everything the goddess was saying. Everything that she had done, every mistake that she had made, danced before her eyes. How could she possibly bear the strain of ruling the entire Mortal Plane? Not since she had been a little girl had she even dreamed of such a thing. And yet, here she was. This time, it was her mother's words about Fiora, not Arran's prophecy that filled her mind.

She was noble and brave, and never ran from a battle.

"I will do it," she said, standing.

"Good," Arra said.

Suddenly, the cell was filled with a blinding light. Ren started to cover her eyes, but something compelled her not to. Above her, floating down from the ceiling, as if it were miles above her head, were three golden-skinned giants, glowing with every color she could imagine. The rainbow of light cascaded off of them, bouncing off the walls of the cell like they were made of polished glass. They were so beautiful that Ren began to cry openly.

Each of the Gods of Light held out their hands toward the Paladin. Ren saw that they had all sliced open their palms, allowing the silver blood from within to flow directly onto the floor. The blood moved toward her as if it were alive, crawling up her bare legs and absorbing into her skin. Then the pain began as she felt the wings bursting from her back. She cried out so loudly that she nearly lost her voice.

Then it was done.

The light faded, and the gods were gone. Ren lay curled on the floor, heaving, her body burning inside and out. Her clothing had fallen off, torn by the fresh wings that now sprouted from her back. The door to her cell was thrown open and the guards rushed in, swords drawn. When they saw her wings, they immediately fell to their knees. Ren stood, towering over them. She felt a new strength surging through her body.

Go to the Cathedral.

Arra spoke within her mind. The voice was almost a part of her now. She could even sense the emotions emitted by each of the three gods. Arra was proud. Samson and Luna were indifferent.

Go to your people.

"Rise," Ren said. "Fetch me a cloak."

THE CENTRAL CHAMBER of the Grand Cathedral was filled beyond capacity. Though many of the pews were still blackened and bloodstained, people from all over Illux had gathered to witness the creation of a new Seraph. Traditionally, this had occurred in private, and none but the new Seraph had laid eyes upon the Gods of Light, but Castille had decried that this was to be as public as possible. He had wished for everyone to see his radiance, tradition be damned. There would be no room for anyone to question his authority after this display.

The old Paladin stood on the central dais, mere paces away from where his presumed predecessor had been killed. He was adorned in a simple white robe, with slits already cut into the back for his new wings to sprout from. A priest stood next to him, leading the gathered congregation in a prayer of supplication to the Gods of Light. None of them noticed the hooded figure that walked barefoot into the crowded room.

Ren walked past the bowed heads of her subjects. Only a few dared to look up and see who it was that disturbed this sacred ceremony. When she was halfway to the dais, Castille noticed her. Though she was hooded, their eyes locked, and his face turned scarlet. The Paladin's hand snapped the holy book the priest was holding shut.

"You dare come here?!" he shouted. "Paladins, arrest this woman! She is the one who betrayed our beloved Seraph. It's her fault that Jerrok lies dead."

Several Paladins stood, drawing weapons. Ren lifted her hands to her hood and lowered it. Gasps sprang from the crowd. Each of the Paladins stopped their approach, mouths agape. Her once black hair was now completely white. Fear crossed Castille's face. Ren didn't slow her walk to the dais.

"It's some kind of trick! She is no Seraph. The Gods of Light would never have chosen a traitor to be their voice."

"They chose Arendt," the priest said.

Castille turned to the man, his fists clenched. Ren reached the dais, climbing the few steps to stand on equal ground with the two men. It was then that she dropped her cloak to the ground, spreading her wings as she did so. Swords clattered onto the ground, and shouts rang out from the congregation. All of those gathered once again fell to their knees.

Ren's gaze fell to Castille. The rage left his face, replaced by true terror. He lowered himself and looked away from her in shame. The priest placed Nightbreaker in her hand. The blade was lighter than she expected. She looked down its length. Her white hair looked so foreign on its surface.

"Long live the Seraph!" someone shouted.

"Long live Ren!" yelled another.

She didn't say a word.

THAT NIGHT, Ren stood alone in the catacombs beneath the city. She was in the most sacred of the burial chambers, reserved only for Seraphs and the greatest heroes of the Light. The newly made Seraph was no longer naked, now wearing armor specially made for her kind. Beside her was Arran, lying peacefully on a raised platform, a silver shroud draped over her body.

This had been her first decree since her appearance before the people of the city: Arran and all of the other Paladins who had died defending the city from the Demon attack were to be given burials with the highest honors. None would question their commitment to the Light. She owed them all that much at least.

Especially you.

When Ren could no longer hear the footsteps of the Paladins who had carried her sister down here, she wept. No one could see her cry anymore. All they could see was strength. It had to be so. She clutched the cold hand of her friend, speaking softly in the darkness.

"I love you," she whispered. "I will see you again one day, sister. Until then, I will not let you down. From these ashes, I will rise to protect our people, just as you said. That will be the true salvation. Not conquest, but defense. I promise that I will put the safety of Illux and the villages above all else. For you."

When she was done, Ren dried her eyes and turned away. After the city recovered from the attack and the change in leadership, she would go to Amel and visit her parents. She needed their counsel now, more than ever. On her walk down to the catacombs, she had decided that she would keep Castille in his current position, at least for the time being. He was too respected and too experienced to simply cast aside. Even though the old man was cruel, and would have executed her just hours ago, he had been following the orders of the Seraph and doing what he thought to be right. She would not punish him for that, so long as he stayed loyal.

As she walked down the dark corridor back toward the steps leading up to the world of light above, she saw the silver shroud that covered Jerrok. The Seraph laid alone in a circular room just off the main passage. Ren passed by without giving him a second glance.

WHAT TO READ NEXT

To follow Ren's continued rule of Illux, read *Wrath of the Fallen.*

To find out the fate of Kane Darksend, read *A Voice from the Darkness* and *The Last Gift of Kane Darksend.*

To learn the origin of the Seraph-blade Nightbreaker, read *The Nightbreaker.*

ABOUT THE AUTHOR

Kris Jerome was born in the middle of a snowstorm in Pendleton, Oregon, several decades ago. Since then he moved the great distance across the state to study at Willamette University. He obtained a BFA in Digital Communication Arts in June of 2016 from Oregon State University. Kris enjoys reading books and comics while sipping wine and craft beer. He currently lives in Albany, Oregon with his wife, seven children and two cats.

darktidingspress.com
darktidingspress@gmail.com

www.ingramcontent.com/pod-product-compliance
Lightning Source LLC
Chambersburg PA
CBHW030532310726
48979CB00010B/1893/J
9781951138097